Larry Potter and The Jungle Mystery

Sd Mikail

ISBN 978-93-5458-271-4
© Sd Mikail 2021
Published in India 2021 by Pencil

A brand of
One Point Six Technologies Pvt. Ltd.
123, Building J2, Shram Seva Premises,
Wadala Truck Terminal, Wadala (E)
Mumbai 400037, Maharashtra, INDIA
E connect@thepencilapp.com
W www.thepencilapp.com

DISCLAIMER: *This is a work of fiction. Names, characters, places, events and incidents are the products of the author's imagination. The opinions expressed in this book do not seek to reflect the views of the Publisher.*

Author biography

Syed Mikail Ali was born on 4th January 1986 and brought up in Birbhum West Bengal. After completing his Graduation (BA Honours in English Literature) started teaching in a private school. He has taught in different states of India and also in Maldives.

Though by profession he is teacher, he has special interest in writing specially fiction and children book.

He is a very good story teller. He loves children.

The author can be reached at +919064930207 (call / whatsapp) or Email - syedmikailali@gmail.com

CONTENTS

Epigraph

Mr. Potter was a famous master of wizardry. He saved Syndriya from the wretched clutches of the dark queen. The King of Syndriya became happy with Mr. Potter and offered the hands of his daughter princess Lyona Waladhee. He taught her magic and witchcraft to control the dark activities of the dark evil queen. The dark queen became very angry with Mr. Potter and was determined to kill him. Mr. Potter had no power to kill the dark queen. So he transmitted special magical power to their upcoming baby by doing some special magical miracle. Meantime the dark queen captured the heart and mind of Anastasiya , Lyona's sister and taught her dark magic and planted jealous enmity in her and tempted her that she will become the queen. The dark queen killed Mr. Potter with the help of Anastasiya. An unending enemity started between the two sisters and the kingdom was divided into two. The supporters of dark power formed Izyndriya, a new kingdom. But the dark queen wanted to kill Lyona who was pregnant. The dark queen with the help of Izyndriya attacked Syndriya many times. Pregnant Lyona faught bravely to save her people. The day she gave birth to Larry there was a great turmoil in her kingdom as a great army was about to attack her. Just after birth she handed over Baby Larry to Mr. and Mrs. Smith, her most faithful servants and instructed to leave the palace as soon as possible. They did so according to the Queen's order. Actually the dark queen wanted to kill the baby girl as she was given special power to kill any evil dark power. So the death of the dark queen was destined in her hand. That's why the dark queen tried with all her might to kill the baby girl.

After her birth her mother was in great problem as the evil eye of dark queen fell on her. She had fight against the dark queen. She became busy in the fight instead of loving her new born baby. Mr. Smith and Mrs. Smith were taking care of the baby but the situation changed as the dark queen attacked her kingdom and destroyed everything. Secretly Mr. Smith and Mrs. Smith escaped to save the baby girl Larry. The dark queen knew her end was in the hand of this baby. Mr and Mrs Smith lived secretly two years a distressful and hard life to save the baby. Her mother was killed by the dark queen and her soul was kept in the rocks in the mountain jungle. Larry suffered hardship from birth.

Chapter 1 The Poor Plight of Larry

A green gloomy ground covered with half yellow and half brown fence and multi-colour feeble flowers strewn over the ground and grey colour small birds that were flying over here and there aimlessly mark the landmark of Mr. Walworth Smith's house. But better to say it is Mrs. Steffina Smilth's house as the latter has much more authority over the former in the house. Mr. Smith prefers to avoid the jerks of daily life due to the bad temper of his wife. So he spends most of his time in his farm. He works in the farm all day long and finds happiness there in spite of hardworking but becomes very sad at home. He has a past that is totally different from his present. It seems that still he lives in his past and he likes it. He spends most of the time in the farm alone and comes home only for meals to fulfil necessary biological onus.

Once he had a lovely home with lot of happiness and he used to lead a labourious luxury life here. But unfortunately his lovely home has turned into a distressful house and luxury has gone from his labourios life. His lovely home had a natural luxury life that all people used to praise but some were jealous of his happy life. Anyway ups and downs are inseparable parts of human life and he is not an exception. After the death of his first wife, Lady Kathelene Smith, he cannot find the happy home that once he had. His second wife, Mrs Steffina Smith, is different from his first wife which he didn't expected even in his dream.

Here lives our little Larry who is talented but gets tortured by her step mother which makes her upset. Though she lives with her parents but her life is no better than an orphan. She has few friends but is always afraid to play with them - even to meet them. She used to go school regularly but she stopped going school due to many reasons. The prime reason is her misfortune. She cannot lead a life of joy and merriment like other children of her age. She has a lot of problems. She is a child without any childhood. In this little age she experienced many great lessons of life. She works like an adult almost. Actually she is leading a very sad and lonely life full of suffering mentally and physically.

The day looks strange due to the competition between the sun and the clouds. A squirrel is trying to get down from the tree but it is afraid of something. The stray dogs were lying lifelessly on the dusty lane. Larry is sitting alone on the ground under the tree with a heavy heart and strange look marking clear signs of sadness over her face but still she tries to look normal. A man enters with slow and shaky steps seems to be very tired and hungry. This is Larry's father Mr Walworth Smith. He stops seeing Larry sitting alone on the ground of his deserted garden. He comes to Larry with slow and silent steps.

"Hey Larry! How is your day?" – He asks Larry making a smile on his fatigued face.

"Oh, Pa, it's good. Yeah it's good." – says Larry hiding something behind her artificial smile.

"Why are you sitting alone?" – he asks casually.

"Just having some fresh air." – she replies.

"How is your new mother now?" – he asks.

"She is very good indeed. She is very nice!" – she replies.

"Well, did you trace any difference between your old mother and this new mother?" – he asks with hesitation and it seems as if he asked by mistake.

"What difference?" – she repeats his question being little puzzled.

"I mean do you find any difference between your mother and this new mother – I mean your step mother?" – he explains the question to her as she was pretending as if she has not understood the question.

"Pa, there is a lot of difference between the two – infact hell and heaven difference!" – she says seriously and her eyes make a different expression.

"What do you mean to say?" – asks the man.

"I mean … ahh .. I mean my old mother - my mother was a liar!" – she says abruptly.

"What? Liar! Your mother was a liar!!" – he asks expressing his surprise.

"Yes Pa, she was a great liar!" – she affirms.

"But how? What did she lie to you?" – he asks eagerly with serious curious eyes.

"When I didn't listen to her, she used to say – 'I will not give you any food today'. When I didn't eat on time or when I became busy with my friends in playing games; she used to tell me that she won't give me food if I don't listen to her. But after sometime she used to search me and forced me to eat and even sometimes she didn't eat anything to feed me. She only used to tell lie that she won't give me food…" – she says with a strange grim look and something chocked her.

"And this mother?" – he asks with creepy curiosity.

"She only speaks the truth." – she says in a grim tone.

"How?" – he asks.

"If I don't listen to her, she tells me that she won't give me food. And indeed she hasn't given me anything to eat since last two days… She does what she says. She is not a liar like my mom." – said Larry to her father. She could not control her emotion. Larry sobbed and tears rolled down on her innocent silky cheeks as she could not stop it. Larry's father also felt very sad. His weary face turned pale. But he was helpless and felt himself guilty for Larry's poor plight.

"I am sorry! I am sorry Larry. It is due to me but I am helpless. I am extremely sorry Larry. Please do listen to her properly and do anything she orders to do. Do everything she asks you to do and do them on time. Please cooperate. Everything will be fine soon." – replied Larry's father in a sad and remorseful tone.

Suddenly a shrill shout was heard. It was Larry's step-mother. She was calling Larry - "Larry! Larry! Laarrryyyy…." – the vociferous voice said.

"Go she is calling you! Go fast! Go and listen to her." – said Larry's father to Larry patting her back to soothe her sad plight vainly. (Larry ran to her step mother)

"Ye … yes mom…" – said Larry with her trembling tongue and she was very nervous as her step mother was looking at her in a very angry mood.

"Where is my stick?" – she asked Larry in a cool and firm voice with a stiff look.

"I … I don't know mom." – replied Larry in a shaking speech being too much afraid.

"You don't know … don't tell lie." – she said in a harsh tone trying to exert her uncontrollable anger.

"Mom! Mom! It's here… it's here... the stick is here!" – shouted a boy from the hall. It was Larry's step young brother, Jacob, who found the stick in the corner of the hall.

"Larry, go and bring the stick to me immediately." – Mrs Steffina ordered with all her majestic power. Larry moved unwillingly at a very slow pace and fear covered her body and soul. She brought the stick and gave it to her step mother reluctantly.

"So like a good girl stretch your both hands right here and show me the palms." She ordered using her authoritative power in the family vested to her the day she married to Mr Wolworth Smith.

Larry knew what was going to happen to her. Might be that she had found another mistake or something wrong with Larry. Obviously she would get punished and there was no way to escape from her punishment. It was a common fact in her fate and almost a daily matter. Larry reluctantly stretched her fearful shaking hands to receive the hard blows on her soft pink palms from her step mother. Her pinkish white palms were trembling and any good hearted person would like to kiss them instead of hurting. But Mrs. Steffina was having a tigress inside her with no feelings and kindness.

"Straight! I say straight!" – shouted Mrs. Steffina ordering Larry to stretch her palms straight.

Being bound by the order Larry reluctantly stretched her hands with open palms. She started showering blows with the stick on Larry's soft palms mercilessly and the house got filled with her helpless cry. (Initially when Mrs. Steffina was beating Larry, her step brother started laughing but soon he became silent and shocked after seeing the violent blows.)

Her father came and rescued Larry from that tigress. Yes she was indeed a ferocious tigress – healthy with a tall and straight figure and wild anger. Larry's father was shorter than her by 2 inch and not so healthy. If a wrestling match is held between the two she would beat him badly.

"Sweet heart, what wrong she has done? Why are you beating her so mercilessly?" – asked Larry's father in a pitiful pleasing voice.

"Wrong! Don't you smell something bad inside the house?" – asked Mrs Steffina angrily.

"Smell! Something bad smell!" – said he with surprise.

"I think you need to clean your nostrils – they must be blocked." – said Mrs Steffina to her husband with a cool and cross look.

"What do you mean?" – he asked her politely trying to please and pacify her.

"I can smell some dead rats are rotting here in our house. I told that nasty girl to find and clean it well. But she went to play with her fowl friends. I told her to stop playing. I told her to find out the dead rats. But she didn't. Instead she went to play. How did she dare to ignore my order?" – she said to him making a bold complain against Larry.

"Darling she is a small girl. It is the age to play and eat. Forgive her. Please have mercy on her. God will bless you. God will have mercy on you." – he requested.

"Mercy! On this filthy witch! Never! If she does all work perfectly so she will be here and might get some food. If she goes to play I will throw her out. If she fails to do the tasks I will never give her a morsel of food. No work no food." – she said to him with a firm and cruel voice raising her ndex finger almost at Mr. Smith's nose making him totally silent.

Suddenly the room becomes silent for a moment. She turns to Larry.

"Is that clear to you?" – she shouted at Larry.

Larry was groaning in pain. Her step mother came and kicked her badly. She fell down on the floor. Her father came and tried to soothe her.

"Hey nasty girl! Get up immediately. Go and find out the dead rats now! Else be ready to face harder punishment." – she shouted at Larry even more loudly.

"Ye… yes mom, I will … I will find it now…" – said Larry with tears in her eyes in painful quivering voice. Larry's father was helpless and he had to watch it. Larry's step brother was feeling hungry. He also got socked after watching the wretched condition of Larry. But he was not able to feel it as he was taught to hate her from the beginning. Mrs. Steffina never allowed him to play with Larry.

"Mom I am feeling hungry. I want to eat something." – said the boy.

"Oh! My dear. You are feeling hungry. Lunch is ready. Let's go to the dining hall to enjoy nice food." – said Mrs Steffina with a loving smile to her son. Mrs. Steffina changed her attitude immediately like weather. When she had to deal with her son she becomes a flower but in case of Larry she turns into a thorn. She showers love on her son but she thunders on Larry. Now you can see a soft tender mother in Mrs. Steffina with unending affection and care as she started showering love on her son.

Larry was watching with her poor pitiful pathetic eyes at her step mother who was loving her step brother affectionately. Larry's heart seemed to be very thirsty –

thirsty of love – thirsty of care – thirsty of affection – thirsty of some sweet lovely words. No words can describe her thirsty face devoid of love and affection. Her heart was longing for sweet words, little care and lot of love. But she was born unfortunate.

***** ((Mr. Potter was a famous master of wizardry. He saved Syndriya from the wretched clutches of the dark queen. The King of Syndriya became happy with Mr. Potter and offered the hands of his daughter princess Lyona Waladhee. He taught her magic and witchcraft to control the dark activities of the dark evil queen. The dark queen became very angry with Mr. Potter and was determined to kill him. Mr. Potter had no power to kill the dark queen. So he transmitted special magical power to their upcoming baby by doing some special magical miracle. Meantime the dark queen captured the heart and mind of Anastasiya , Lyona's sister and taught her dark magic and planted jealous enmity in her and tempted her that she will become the queen. The dark queen killed Mr. Potter with the help of Anastasiya. An unending enemity started between the two sisters and the kingdom was divided into two. The supporters of dark power formed Izyndriya, a new kingdom. But the dark queen wanted to kill Lyona who was pregnant. The dark queen with the help of Izyndriya attacked Syndriya many times. Pregnant Lyona faught bravely to save her people. The day she gave birth to Larry there was a great turmoil in her kingdom as a great army was about to attack her. Just after birth she handed over Baby Larry to Mr. and Mrs. Smith, her most faithful servants and instructed to leave the palace as soon as possible. They did so according to the Queen's order. Actually the dark queen wanted to kill the baby girl as she was given special power to kill any evil dark power. So the death of the dark queen was destined in her hand. That's why the dark queen tried with all her might to kill the baby girl.

After her birth her mother was in great problem as the evil eye of dark queen fell on her. She had fight against the dark queen. She became busy in the fight instead of loving her new born baby. Mr. Smith and Mrs. Smith were taking care of the baby but the situation changed as the dark queen attacked her kingdom and destroyed everything. Secretly Mr. Smith and Mrs. Smith escaped to save the baby girl Larry. The dark queen knew her end was in the hand of this baby. Mr and Mrs Smith lived secretly two years a distressful and hard life to save the baby. Her mother was killed by the dark queen and her soul was kept in the rocks in the mountain jungle. Larry suffered hardship from birth.))

"Don't waste time. Go and find the dead rotten rats immediately. I don't want to listen any excuse. Do you understand that?" – she barked at Larry before stepping out of the room. Larry's step mother went for lunch with her son and called Larry's father also. Larry's father was not that much powerful to overrule his second wife. It was better for him to listen to her. There was a secret between the two and that's why Larry's father never dared to say a word against his wife – whether she did right or wrong he had to nod his head with a 'yes' … and always he had to do so.

A green gloomy ground covered with half yellow and half brown fence and multi-colour feeble flowers strewn over the ground and grey colour small birds that were flying over here and there aimlessly mark the landmark of Mr.

Walworth Smith's house. But better to say it is Mrs. Steffina Smilth's house as the latter has much more authority over the former in the house. Mr. Smith prefers to avoid the jerks of daily life due to the bad temper of his wife. So he spends most of his time in his farm. He works in the farm all day long and finds happiness there in spite of hardworking but becomes very sad at home. He has a past that is totally different from his present. It seems that still he lives in his past and he likes it. He spends most of the time in the farm alone and comes home only for meals to fulfil necessary biological onus.

Once he had a lovely home with lot of happiness and he used to lead a labourious luxury life here. But unfortunately his lovely home has turned into a distressful house and luxury has gone from his labourios life. His lovely home had a natural luxury life that all people used to praise but some were jealous of his happy life. Anyway ups and downs are inseparable parts of human life and he is not an exception. After the death of his first wife, Lady Kathelene Smith, he cannot find the happy home that once he had. His second wife, Mrs Steffina Smith, is different from his first wife which he didn't expected even in his dream.

Here lives our little Larry who is talented but gets tortured by her step mother which makes her upset. Though she lives with her parents but her life is no better than an orphan. She has few friends but is always afraid to play with them - even to meet them. She used to go school regularly but she stopped going school due to many reasons. The prime reason is her misfortune. She cannot lead a life of joy and merriment like other children of her age. She has a lot of problems. She is a child without any childhood. In this little age she experienced many great lessons of life. She works like an adult almost. Actually she is leading a very sad and lonely life full of suffering mentally and physically.

The day looks strange due to the competition between the sun and the clouds. A squirrel is trying to get down from the tree but it is afraid of something. The stray dogs were lying lifelessly on the dusty lane. Larry is sitting alone on the ground under the tree with a heavy heart and strange look marking clear signs of sadness over her face but still she tries to look normal. A man enters with slow and shaky steps seems to be very tired and hungry. This is Larry's father Mr Walworth Smith. He stops seeing Larry sitting alone on the ground of his deserted garden. He comes to Larry with slow and silent steps.

"Hey Larry! How is your day?" – He asks Larry making a smile on his fatigued face.

"Oh, Pa, it's good. Yeah it's good." – says Larry hiding something behind her artificial smile.

"Why are you sitting alone?" – he asks casually.

"Just having some fresh air." – she replies.

"How is your new mother now?" – he asks.

"She is very good indeed. She is very nice!" – she replies.

"Well, did you trace any difference between your old mother and this new mother?" – he asks with hesitation and it seems as if he asked by mistake.

"What difference?" – she repeats his question being little puzzled.

"I mean do you find any difference between your mother and this new mother – I mean your step mother?" – he explains the question to her as she was pretending as if she has not understood the question.

"Pa, there is a lot of difference between the two – infact hell and heaven difference!" – she says seriously and her eyes make a different expression.

"What do you mean to say?" – asks the man.

"I mean … ahh .. I mean my old mother - my mother was a liar!" – she says abruptly.

"What? Liar! Your mother was a liar!!" – he asks expressing his surprise.

"Yes Pa, she was a great liar!" – she affirms.

"But how? What did she lie to you?" – he asks eagerly with serious curious eyes.

"When I didn't listen to her, she used to say – 'I will not give you any food today'. When I didn't eat on time or when I became busy with my friends in playing games; she used to tell me that she won't give me food if I don't listen to her. But after sometime she used to search me and forced me to eat and even sometimes she didn't eat anything to feed me. She only used to tell lie that she won't give me food…" – she says with a strange grim look and something chocked her.

"And this mother?" – he asks with creepy curiosity.

"She only speaks the truth." – she says in a grim tone.

"How?" – he asks.

"If I don't listen to her, she tells me that she won't give me food. And indeed she hasn't given me anything to eat since last two days… She does what she says. She is not a liar like my mom." – said Larry to her father. She could not control her emotion. Larry sobbed and tears rolled down on her innocent silky cheeks as she could not stop it. Larry's father also felt very sad. His weary face turned pale. But he was helpless and felt himself guilty for Larry's poor plight.

"I am sorry! I am sorry Larry. It is due to me but I am helpless. I am extremely sorry Larry. Please do listen to her properly and do anything she orders to do. Do everything she asks you to do and do them on time. Please cooperate. Everything will be fine soon." – replied Larry's father in a sad and remorseful tone.

Suddenly a shrill shout was heard. It was Larry's step-mother. She was calling Larry - "Larry! Larry! Laarrryyyy...." – the vociferous voice said.

"Go she is calling you! Go fast! Go and listen to her." – said Larry's father to Larry patting her back to soothe her sad plight vainly. (Larry ran to her step mother)

"Ye ... yes mom..." – said Larry with her trembling tongue and she was very nervous as her step mother was looking at her in a very angry mood.

"Where is my stick?" – she asked Larry in a cool and firm voice with a stiff look.

"I ... I don't know mom." – replied Larry in a shaking speech being too much afraid.

"You don't know ... don't tell lie." – she said in a harsh tone trying to exert her uncontrollable anger.

"Mom! Mom! It's here... it's here... the stick is here!" – shouted a boy from the hall. It was Larry's step young brother, Jacob, who found the stick in the corner of the hall.

"Larry, go and bring the stick to me immediately." – Mrs Steffina ordered with all her majestic power. Larry moved unwillingly at a very slow pace and fear covered her body and soul. She brought the stick and gave it to her step mother reluctantly.

"So like a good girl stretch your both hands right here and show me the palms." She ordered using her authoritative power in the family vested to her the day she married to Mr Wolworth Smith.

Larry knew what was going to happen to her. Might be that she had found another mistake or something wrong with Larry. Obviously she would get punished and there was no way to escape from her punishment. It was a common fact in her fate and almost a daily matter. Larry reluctantly stretched her fearful shaking hands to receive the hard blows on her soft pink palms from her step mother. Her pinkish white palms were trembling and any good hearted person would like to kiss them instead of hurting. But Mrs. Steffina was having a tigress inside her with no feelings and kindness.

"Straight! I say straight!" – shouted Mrs. Steffina ordering Larry to stretch her palms straight.

Being bound by the order Larry reluctantly stretched her hands with open palms. She started showering blows with the stick on Larry's soft palms mercilessly and the house got filled with her helpless cry. (Initially when Mrs. Steffina was beating Larry, her step brother started laughing but soon he became silent and shocked after seeing the violent blows.)

Her father came and rescued Larry from that tigress. Yes she was indeed a ferocious tigress – healthy with a tall and straight figure and wild anger. Larry's father was shorter than her by 2 inch and not so healthy. If a wrestling match is held between the two she would beat him badly.

"Sweet heart, what wrong she has done? Why are you beating her so mercilessly?" – asked Larry's father in a pitiful pleasing voice.

"Wrong! Don't you smell something bad inside the house?" – asked Mrs Steffina angrily.

"Smell! Something bad smell!" – said he with surprise.

"I think you need to clean your nostrils – they must be blocked." – said Mrs Steffina to her husband with a cool and cross look.

"What do you mean?" – he asked her politely trying to please and pacify her.

"I can smell some dead rats are rotting here in our house. I told that nasty girl to find and clean it well. But she went to play with her fowl friends. I told her to stop playing. I told her to find out the dead rats. But she didn't. Instead she went to play. How did she dare to ignore my order?" – she said to him making a bold complain against Larry.

"Darling she is a small girl. It is the age to play and eat. Forgive her. Please have mercy on her. God will bless you. God will have mercy on you." – he requested.

"Mercy! On this filthy witch! Never! If she does all work perfectly so she will be here and might get some food. If she goes to play I will throw her out. If she fails to do the tasks I will never give her a morsel of food. No work no food." – she said to him with a firm and cruel voice raising her ndex finger almost at Mr. Smith's nose making him totally silent.

Suddenly the room becomes silent for a moment. She turns to Larry.

"Is that clear to you?" – she shouted at Larry.

Larry was groaning in pain. Her step mother came and kicked her badly. She fell down on the floor. Her father came and tried to soothe her.

"Hey nasty girl! Get up immediately. Go and find out the dead rats now! Else be ready to face harder punishment." – she shouted at Larry even more loudly.

"Ye... yes mom, I will ... I will find it now..." – said

Larry with tears in her eyes in painful quivering voice. Larry's father was helpless and he had to watch it. Larry's step brother was feeling hungry. He also got socked after watching the wretched condition of Larry. But he was not able to feel it as he was taught to hate her from the beginning. Mrs. Steffina never allowed him to play with Larry.

"Mom I am feeling hungry. I want to eat something." – said the boy.

"Oh! My dear. You are feeling hungry. Lunch is ready. Let's go to the dining hall to enjoy nice food." – said Mrs Steffina with a loving smile to her son. Mrs. Steffina changed her attitude immediately like weather. When she had to deal with her son she becomes a flower but in case of Larry she turns into a thorn. She showers love on her son but she thunders on Larry. Now you can see a soft tender mother in Mrs. Steffina with unending affection and care as she started showering love on her son.

Larry was watching with her poor pitiful pathetic eyes at her step mother who was loving her step brother affectionately. Larry's heart seemed to be very thirsty – thirsty of love – thirsty of care – thirsty of affection – thirsty of some sweet lovely words. No words can describe her thirsty face devoid of love and affection. Her heart was longing for sweet words, little care and lot of love. But she was born unfortunate.

"Don't waste time. Go and find the dead rotten rats immediately. I don't want to listen any excuse. Do you understand that?" – she barked at Larry before stepping out of the room. Larry's step mother went for lunch with her son and called Larry's father also. Larry's father was not that much powerful to overrule his second wife. It was better for him to listen to her. There was a secret between the two and that's why Larry's father never dared to say a word against his wife – whether she did right or wrong he had to nod his head with a 'yes' … and always he had to do so.

Chapter 2 The Rotten Rat and The Nymph

Larry got up with great difficulty and went to search the dead rats. She was hungry, tired and wounded. After facing such insult every day, she has forgotten to feel. She started searching the rat. After searching a lot she could not find any dead rat as her eyes were full of tears. She was not able to see properly. Suddenly she heard some sound but could not understand what the sound was. She ignored it. A small creature most probably a nymph brought the dead rat to her and hushed -

"Laarryy, it is here. The dead rat is here."

Larry got confused after listening the soft sound of the nymph more clearly as she could not find who was saying that. She was looking here and there. But she could not see any one. She was feeling strange as no one was there but still the clear sound was ringing in her ears. Actually she was very down in dumps due to her failure to find out the dead rat.

"Look down here I am standing here in front of you." – said the nymph helping Larry to locate him.

Larry started looking at that point rubbing her eyes. She became afraid after seeing a strange little creature but it indicated to her not to be afraid. It was also feeling sad for the pathetic condition of Larry.

"I am very sad to see you crying. I am your friend. I will help you. She won't be able to beat you anymore. And I will teach your step brother a proper lesson – he will never dare to laugh at you." - said the tiny strange creature to Larry in a polite and pleasing manner and handed over the mouse-trap with the dead rat to Larry.

Larry saw a dead rat almost started getting rotten inside the mouse-trapping box. The rat got a deadly death as its head was badly pressed by that mouse-trapping machine. Still tears were dropping from her lovely innocent eyes. Larry was feeling very hungry. Suddenly a drop of Larry's tears fell on the dead rat and a surprisingly strange thing happened - it became alive … the dead rotten rat became alive. Larry was also surprised to see this. She was totally confused but the nymph was as usual. Adding to her surprise the rat started speaking with Larry from inside the mouse-trapping box in a grateful tone –

"Thank you very much Larry. You have saved my life. I will remain ever grateful to you. Please free me from this cage. I am your friend. I came to meet you." – said the dead rat politely to win pity from Larry.

"Strange! Rats can speak. I cannot believe it." - Larry spoke to herself. Nice smell of food was coming as they were having lunch in the dining hall. Larry was not allowed to eat with them. She could not go and join them. She didn't dare to go inside the hall. But she could not enjoy the smell. She was very much hungry as she was not given any food by her step mother for last two days. She was terribly longing for food. She tried to console her stomach with the good smell of the food. And indeed the smell of nice food from the dining hall smoothed her appetite.

"Larry please take me out! Free me soon! Please! Free me.

I am your friend. Free me." – the rat urged madly.

"Ok I will do that. I will free you. But I have a condition." – said Larry.

"Condition! What is your condition?" – asked the rat.

"You just pretend to be dead for few more moments." - said Larry purposefully.

"Why? Why should I pretend to be dead while I am not?" asked the rat wisely.

"I will inform my mom that I have found the dead rat. So she might be happy and may give me some food if she shows little mercy on me." – said Larry in a very sad tone.

"That's ok but how can I? How can I be dead or pretend to be dead again?" – said the rat silently in a reluctant tone showing its unwillingness to be dead again.

The nymph felt like crying after listening the pathetic situation of Larry. The nymph with its magic power instantly made the rat dead again – a rotten one with bad smell.

Larry became happy as she could show her mother that she had found the dead rat. She might be pleased at her task of finding dead rotten rat and might give her some food. So she went to her mom to show that dead rat inside the cage.

"Mom I have found it – here is the dead rat. It has started getting rotten." - she informed with an artificial smile. But again bad luck! She expected her step mother would be happy and might appreciate her effort to find out the dead rotten rat. But instead she became very angry and started shouting at Larry with her shrill sound -

"You filthy bitch! Don't you see we are having lunch? How dare you to bring that filthy thing here? Go and throw it in the bush outside the house. Get lost now! Get out of here immediately!" – she shouted at Larry again more furiously.

Her step brother threw a spoon to hit her but it hit him back as the nymph did something. Otherwise it would have hit her badly. She moved with a sad heart and tearful eyes with the dead rat and went to a bush outside her house. She was sad as her plan failed again. She was now totally down in the dumps. But the rat was dead whom she told to pretend to be dead. She shook the cage to awake the dead rat but it didn't. She tried again and the result was same. The nymph could not be seen anywhere.

"How can I make it alive again? After all it is my friend." She spoke to herself.

"Larry … Larry, come inside the bush." - a voice called her. She is very much scared as the voice was coarse and bizarre. She stood there being afraid and confused.

'Don't be scared we are your friends. Come inside the bush." - the voice said politely and it was charming also. Larry felt something was attracting her like a magnet.

She went inside. A group of tadpoles and rats were waiting for Larry. As she entered the bush they all stood up and bowed down before Larry in an awful respect.

"Oh Miss Larry Potter, the Ever Best Witch of the world! The superior one! We are your slaves – order us anything, we will do for you." - said one of the rats.

"Excuse me. I am Larry Smith – not Larry Potter. Strange! I cannot understand what you mean to say." - said Larry being totally confused after seeing rats and tadpoles talking in groups.

"It is not strange. We never make mistake. You don't know who you are. Please make our Joe alive again." - requested one of the tadpoles.

"Joe! Who is Joe?" - asked Larry with astonishment.

"That dead rat! He is our friend Joe." - said another rat.

"But how can I make a dead rotten rat alive again. I don't know how to make it alive again. I cannot do it." - denied Larry. Larry was feeling irritating and puzzled.

"Oh Great Larry Potter you can do it. You can bring back life to any dead creature – you are blessed with great magical power – you are the Ever Best Witch of the World." - said an old rat with an awesome smile of praise.

"Witch! I am a witch!" - exclaimed Larry with anger and astonishment.

"Yes you are – the good one. You are the ever best witch of the world" - said another tadpole.

"I think you must be having wrong information about me. I am Larry Smith. I am not a witch. Why don't you understand that?" - said Larry with a strong feeling of irritation.

 (She got confused and started crying being unable to understand what these rats and tadpoles were saying. As she was crying a drop of her tear fell down on the dead rotten rat from her eyes. As soon as it fell on the dead rat it woke up – it became alive again.)

"Thank you Miss Larry Potter for saving my life once again." - said the rat from the cage in a cool mood.

Larry was surprised to see the dead rat became alive again and speaking to her. She thought that it had happened that time due to that nymph but now how did this happen. She was in confusion.

"How do you become alive again?" - asked Larry to that rat curiously.

"It is you who made me alive again." - replied the rat.

"Me?" - asked Larry being totally tangled.

"Yes Miss Great Larry Potter. It is you who made me alive again." – the rat replied politely.

'Strange! But how do I do that and when?" - asked Larry with strange curiosity.

"Just now you did this. Your tears have special healing power – it can bring life back to any dead corpse. You can make any dead creature alive again." - said the old rat.

"Oh really! I don't know that." asked Larry with a curved joking tone.

"Please free me from this cage. Your mother must be waiting for you to get the dirty plates washed as she has finished lunch. Please free me and go." - requested the rat.

Larry released the rat from the cage. As soon as she freed the rat, all rats and tadpoles got disappeared. She was utterly muddled. She remained stunned for a moment after seeing all these events. She returned home with a sad and jumbled mind. She was also feeling very hungry. She was hopeful that her mother would give her something to eat. But her fate was different. As usual her mother was waiting with the stick like an angry wolf. She was ready to punish her as Larry spoilt her lunch with the bad smell of that nasty rotten rat. Her step brother vomited and so did her father. Larry stepped to her slowly expecting few more blows from her.

"Good girl. Very good girl. So you don't know that when people are having lunch you must not bring any rotten thing as it spoils the meal." - said the heartless lady crushing both the jaws in cool anger.

"Sorry mom, I … I will never do that again. I am extremely sorry mom. Please forgive me." - Larry pleaded and fell down on her feet.

But Larry was not able to melt her stone heart. She tried to beat her but could not beat. She tried her best but she could not beat rather she had hit herself with that stick. The more she tried to hit Larry the more she hit herself. (The nymph was doing something with its magical power and saved Larry from being beaten by her cruel step mother.)

"You nasty witch get out of here, go and clean the dirty plates." – she roared smashing her teeth to control her uncontrollable wrath.

Larry ran to clean the dirty plates. She saw some left over foods in the dirty plates and she didn't stop herself from eating those filthy foods to fill her stomach. But it was not sufficient. The nymph came and cleaned all dirty plates in a moment with its magic power.

"I have to speak with you Larry something serious." - said the Nymph to her in a whisper.

"Something serious! What do you mean? And who are you?" - asked Larry inquisitively.

"I am your friend. I am your servant." - said the nymph.

"My friend! My servant! You are my friend?" - exclaimed Larry in a strange manner.

"I will come back later and tell you details. See you soon." - the Nymph said and got vanished.

"How much time do you need to wash those plates? Do it faster. The dining table is giving very bad smell. They have vomited on it and due to you only this happened." – shouted Mrs Steffina from the hall.

"Sorry mom, I will never repeat that … I will never commit that mistake." – apologized Larry in a soft tone.

"Stop jabbering just wash the plates fast and clean the dining table quickly." – she roared standing near the door.

"Yes mom I will do it right now." - replied Larry.

As the nymph already cleaned the plates, Larry kept the cleaned plates on the right place and went to her mother.

"Mom I have cleaned all the plates." - Larry informed her mother.

"Ok then…" - her mother wanted to say something.

"Mo … mom … may I have something to eat. I am very hungry – very hungry. Please give me something to eat as soon as possible." - requested Larry with her timid tone.

"Food! How do you dare to ask for food! Remember - no work no food. And learn to behave properly. Learn the good manners." - her step mother roared.

"Mom, please give something…." - pleaded Larry being unable to bear the fire of hunger in her stomach.

"Ok I will … I will give you food but first you clean the dining table. Clean it properly as Jacob had vomited over it. Go and do that fast." - she ordered with a curved face.

"Yes mom I will do it now…" replied Larry.

The table was giving very bad smell as her step brother vomited over it. Larry cleaned it quickly.

"Mom the table is cleaned." - said Larry.

"Oh! Ok wait. Here is some food and don't eat it here. Go to your room and eat there." - said her step mother and gave her some food.

Larry's face was getting to be bright after seeing the food and became happy to get it.

"Thank you very much mom… thank you." - said Larry with a prompt artificial smile.

"It's okay. Go. Get lost." - her mother replied carelessly.

Larry left the hall and straight walked towards her room.

Chapter 3 Greymalkin, The Black Cat

Larry went to her room. Room! It was a small and dark store room inside the stable. She had no room in the house. When she was very small she used to pass urine sometimes in the house and it was unbearable for Mrs. Steffina, her step mother. So she shifted her to the stable – hardly suitable for humans to live specially for a child. She was only five years old then. She was afraid to live here alone as it was dark. But someone was always with her with an unseen lamp of love to console her and to help her. Larry used to feel a silence presence of someone who used to soothe her in her poor plight. Larry gradually became used to with it.

Larry sat on the floor and started eating. Oh! It was bad food – it was some stale food. Slight bad smell was coming. She was not given any fresh food by her. She was still eating it as she was very hungry.

"Larry… Larry… Larrryyyy…." called her mother with her usual high pitch sound.

Larry just started to eat but she was calling. Ignoring her hunger, Larry left the food uncovered and ran to her.

"Ye.. ye.. yes mom…" – asked Larry with a great sigh.

"Are you deaf? Can't you listen that I am calling you? How much louder should I shout to call you?" – she asked with her usual angry tone.

"Sorry mom…" – replied Larry in an apologizing way.

"Stop nonsense! Go and clean the floor. Jacob has just passed urine. Do it immediately." – she ordered.

"Yes mom… sure I will…." – assured Larry politely.

Larry started cleaning the floor. After finishing, she went back to her room to eat that stale food. But alas! A cat had eaten all her food. It was a black cat. After eating that food it was sitting there bravely. Larry came and found no food in her plate. She saw that cat and understood who had eaten her food.

"You black moggy – you have eaten my food! What should I eat now? I am hungry – I have nothing to eat." – cried Larry.

"Sorry Larry. I was also hungry. I could not stop myself to eat your food. I was very hungry. I am so sorry Larry." – replied the black cat making Larry more puzzled.

"You can talk … you can understand me." – asked Larry.

"Yes I can talk. Forgive me Great Miss Larry Potter. I am sorry. I have eaten your food. I am bit old and lazy and cannot catch rats. Nowadays rats are too smart. It is very difficult to catch one." – said the black cat in a cool tone.

"Who are you?" – asked Larry out of curiosity.

"I am Greymalkin, a witch. In fact I am your friend. I am your servant. I am always ready to serve you, Great Miss Larry Potter." – said the black cat.

"Greymalkin! I haven't heard this name before. And I don't know any witch." – replied Larry surprisingly.

"You are right Larry. How will you hear my name? I was in captivity. Just now I manage to flee." – replied the black cat.

"In captivity!" – exclaimed Larry being more puzzled.

"Yes I was in captivity." – replied the black cat casually.

"But where? Who captured you?" – asked Larry.

"Don't ask that question again. We don't mention her name. She is the queen of Black World. She is very powerful. We don't utter her name." – said the black cat.

"Queen of Black World!" – exclaimed Larry.

"Yes she is the Queen of Black World." – replied the black cat expressing her fear.

"What are you saying? I cannot get you." – asked Larry. Larry got bamboozled after hearing those phrases 'captivity', 'queen of Black world', 'we don't utter her name' …

"Tonight you will understand everything. Malmossie will come to meet you when the clock will strike twelve at night." – replied the black cat trying to soothe Larry's thirst of curiosity.

"Malmossie! Night twelve!" – exclaimed Larry again in utmost confusion.

"Don't get scared. Your old friends, your servants, your well-wishers, your protectors, your guardians will come to meet you tonight – to delight you." – replied the black cat.

"But I don't know any of them. I have no well-wishers. I have no servants – no protectors. I am born cursed. I cannot find fortune. What are you saying – it is making me confused." – replied Larry in a sad tone.

"Relax Larry…. Relax. Everything will be clear soon to you. Nothing will remain confusing within you. Just relax Great Miss Larry Potter." – said the black cat.

The cat found beaten marks on her hand and came near to her. Larry got afraid.

"Don't be afraid Larry. After all we are your friends. I can see this beaten mark in your hand and it is giving pain to me – it doesn't suit on your body – none can touch you except that..." – said the black cat.

"Except … who… who is that?" – asked Larry being more curious.

"Sorry Larry we don't mention her name but we all understand who is she, you also must not mention her name just understand – the Queen of Black World … the ever thirsty swine of blood and flesh." – said the black cat.

"Why don't we utter her name?" – asked Larry.

"The more we utter her name, the more powerful she becomes. Words have lot of power." – said the black cat in a grim voice.

"Really you are making a mess in mind – what you are saying I cannot understand – it is beyond my … beyond my understanding." – said a more confused Larry.

"Just relax Larry. Tonight you will understand everything. See you tonight in the great feast." – said the black cat and was ready to disappear.

"Great feast!" – exclaimed Larry.

"Oh yeah! It is a great feast. Tonight you will complete nine and tomorrow you will become 10 years old. More revelations will come to you. Just be ready for the feast." – replied the black cat.

"Tonight I will complete nine …" – started Larry.

"Yes Larry we will celebrate your happy birthday tonight." – said the black cat with a smoky smile.

"My birthday … my birthday celebration. Is it real! Am I in dream? I cannot believe this. Who will celebrate my birthday? I have none. I am alone. I am born cursed. I am born to be oppressed. I am born to get beaten day and night… " – continued Larry being totally puzzled.

"Relax Larry, relax. Your bad days are over. Tonight you will meet your friends and your servants …" – replied the black cat in a polite and soothing voice.

Suddenly some coarse sound is heard but it is very familiar to Larry -

"Larry… Larry… Larrryyy …"

"Oh! It's mom. She is calling me. I must go now." – said Larry with a hasty voice.

"Yeah you must go." – said the cat and got vanished. Larry was surprised to see this – the black cat got disappeared in front of her eyes. She felt totally confused – she was not able to understand what was happening with her. But she had to attend her mother. Larry ran to her mother carrying a great chaos in her mind.

"Larry, immediately go and bring the lambs back to the farm before the sunset and make sure that you won't play with anyone. Don't forget that. Now go and bring them to the farm shed from the field as soon as possible." – ordered her mother

"Ye… yes mom I will go and bring them to the farm now." – said Larry and left immediately to bring the lambs back to the farm.

Chapter 4 The Three Witches and The Wolf

Larry's family had a farm in the outskirt of the village where her father used to work and spent most of the time. But due to his long absence it was not in its old glorious condition. Now he started working again here. There he grew different vegetables. When Larry was passing the farm, she could see her father busy in the farm. She went to the field to bring her lambs back to the farm. Larry lived in a beautiful enchanting village. It was situated in the lap of a mountain. A very nice stream flew beside the village. The village had the mountain in its north and the river in its south and vast green land stretched on its east and west. But the land was not always a blessing for the villagers as the unavailability of water due to the lack of rain and it was a great problem. The beautiful river also remained dry most of the time. The mountain was fully covered with dense forest and became the abode of evil things – bad witches were living there. Different wild animals were also living there. Sometimes the villagers were in need to go to the mountain to collect medicinal plants, honey or wood and many accidents had happened in the past. Many people had lost their lives. The mountain was a cursed one. After sunset no people dared to go near the mountain. Many times the witches attacked the villagers and looted them. A wise spook saved the village from those evil things and drew a safety line around the village to protect it. But it was said that the line would lose its power when villagers would become dishonest – domestic violence will increase, people will become greedy and justice will not be present in the village. One girl will be born in the village with special magical power and she will remove the curse from the mountain. People are waiting for her arrival from many years. But they don't have any idea when she will be born in this village. Still people believe in the old saying and they are waiting for that girl. Larry also knows the story but she does not know that she is that girl.

Larry arrived in the field. There was vast dry land and nothing grew here except wild grass. So people used to bring their horses, cows, goats, lambs to graze here. Most of the time they left their cattle in the field to stay and graze full day and in the afternoon they took them back to the farm. Larry was little late. Other villagers had taken back their cattle as it was a rule all the villagers were following from ages to take back their cattle before the sunset. The sun was almost going to set in a moment. Larry started running to bring her lambs back but she was not able to run fast as she was hungry and was feeling weak also. Finally she found her six lambs and they were grazing near the mountain beyond that safety line. She ran to bring them back but a wolf came and pounced on one lamb and ran away with it inside the mountain jungle. Suddenly black clouds covered the sky and thundering started and seemed that a heavy rain and storm was about to come. Larry was totally afraid. But she was much more afraid of her mother as she would kill her if she could not take all six lambs back to the farm. She was so afraid that she started crying bitterly. Her tears fell on her wounded hand and the wound got cured immediately with a bright light without her notice. It became dark due to the black clouds. Suddenly she heard a sound –

"Don't cry. Don't cry Great Miss Larry Potter. Order us. We are your servants. We are your friends. Don't cry. Don't cry Great Larry Potter. How can we help you?"

Larry could hear the sound but could not see anyone. She became surprised and felt puzzled.

"Who are you?" – demanded Larry partly being afraid and partly being puzzled.

"We are your friends. We are your servants." – said the voice in chorus.

"My friends! My servants!" – said Larry surprisingly.

"Yes we are." – replied the voice in chorus.

"Who are you? Where are you?" – asked Larry.

With a flash of light appeared three witches in their original ugly shape bowing to Larry in respect. Larry became afraid and amazed.

"I am not your friend. Get lost from here." – said Larry.

"Don't misunderstand Great Larry Potter. We are indeed your friends – your servants. Order us anything. Our service is always ready for you." – said one of them.

They started approaching near Larry – tried to come very close to her. But Larry stepped back being afraid of them.

"Oh Great Larry please don't be afraid of us … we are none but your friends. Believe us … trust us" – said the witches in chorus in an innocent and pleasing voice.

Larry dared to face them and stopped stepping back. One by one they touched the feet of Larry and kissed them with great love and respect.

"At last we find our hope." - said the first witch.

"Our savior!" - said the second witch.

"Our protector!" - said the third witch.

"Hope! Savior! Protector!" – murmured Larry being utterly confused with their words and actions.

"Yes you are our hope, you are our savior and you are our protector indeed." – said the witches together.

Larry remained standing silently and was looking gloomy.

"Miss Larry, you are looking very sad. What's wrong with you?" - asked the first witch with a loving voice.

"One wolf has taken one of my lambs. I cannot return home without that. My mother will kill me if I cannot return home with all six lambs." – said Larry desolately.

"It's a very easy task for you to get the lamb back. The wolf may have not seen you otherwise it won't dare to take your lamb. Or it may be that the hungry wolf didn't recognize you." - said the second witch.

"Hungry! Me too very hungry!" – said Larry in a strange way exerting her anger, fear and sadness.

"Oh! Sorry your highness Great Larry Potter. Right now we don't have anything to offer you but tonight we will come to you just after the clock strikes twelve at mid night. We will celebrate your birthday. You are going to complete nine and you will turn ten tonight. Happy birthday Great Miss Larry Potter in advance." - said the third witch.

"My birthday?" – asked Larry.

"Yes it is your birthday. Tonight we will celebrate your birthday party. A grand party!" – said the second witch proudly.

"Really!" – asked Larry with surprise.

"Yes. Now order us what we have to do." – said the first witch.

"Bring my lamb back from that wolf. I want it now. I want

it alive." – ordered Larry.

"Sure we will Great Larry. Just wait here for a moment. We will bring that wolf and you will get your lamb back." – said the third witch with confidence.

"Ikkra Ikkra! Mishara Mishara! Dhikkara Dhikkara!" – the witches uttered weird spells and got vanished in a moment in front of Larry. Larry cannot believe her own eyes and became totally confused.

Wind started blowing and its speed was increasing and it was totally dark - black … black … black.

The witches returned with that wolf. The wolf was looking very ferocious but as soon he saw Larry it became very polite and fell on her feet and kissed them.

"Forgive me Great Larry. I am sorry. I have eaten your lamb. Please forgive me." – said the wolf in a tone of being ashamed and was regretting for causing distress to Larry.

Larry was surprised to see that the wolf was talking like a human and it knew her name too. She was feeling totally confused.

"No problem you just vomit it – we will make it alive again." - said the first witch in a commanding manner.

Larry started sobbing as she was afraid of her mother and it was getting too dark. One of the witch brought a leaf and gave it to the wolf and said –

"Chew this leaf. After chewing this leaf you will feel vomiting."

The wolf started chewing the leaf and soon started vomiting the lamb and finally the eaten flesh of the lamb came out in its worst condition. One of the witches brought the leftover body parts of the lamb from the jungle. Another witch collected tears from Larry's cheeks that was rolling down from her wet eyes as she was sobbing. The third witch asked Larry to sprinkle her tears over the dead lamb's flesh wishing it to be alive. Larry did so and in a moment the pieces of flesh formed the full body of the lamb and it became alive and started bleating. The other lambs also came near it after getting back their fellow friend. Larry got back all her six lambs and she was feeling happy but she could not show her happiness as she was confused with all these things.

"Larry now be happy and smile." – said the third witch.

"Larry, please laugh a little." – requested the second witch.

"The more you laugh, the curse will become weaker." – said the first witch in a wise manner.

"I cannot laugh! I cannot smile! I am born unfortunate! I want to laugh – I want to smile, but I cannot do that. I cannot do that….." - Larry sobbed.

"Don't cry Miss Larry. We are here – we are your friends - your servants. We will remove all your troubles … we will eliminate all pains from you …. One day you will be happy." – said the witches hoping the best to come in Larry's life.

"Who are you actually? I am confused!" – asked Larry.

"I am Hecate" – said the first witch.

"I am Kirke." – said the second witch.

"I am Lilura." – said the third witch.

"Shshh! Someone is coming from the village." – said Hecate and warned other witches and they all got vanished. A human sound is heard.

"Larry! ... Larry! … Laarrie! …" Larry heard her father who came to search her.

"Oh Great Larry please forgive me! Pardon me! I will never repeat this mistake of eating your lambs." - said the wolf and ran into the mountain jungle.

Larry could feel the presence of strange beings around her and she could hear the howling sound of wild animals. But the thundering sound was much louder.

Immediately Larry ran with her lambs and entered the safety line drawn by the wise spook around the village bordering between the jungle and the village. She met her father who was searching her –

"Where were you Larry?" – asked her father lovingly in haste.

"I came to take these lambs." – replied Larry in a tired and chocked voice.

"Let's run home. Rain and storm are going to start soon." – said her father.

They started running through the dark path. Larry forgot her hunger and weakness – anyhow she was running to avoid thunder and heavy rain. Finally they came back home. Heavy rain and storm followed them. Larry could hear the deafening sound of thundering. After many years it started raining in Larry's village. Many years over – it did not rain … the village became dry. This rain might bring new hope and happiness in the village.

Chapter 5 Marolina Reveals a Secret

As usual her angry mother shouted at her without any reasons as it became her habit. After half an hour the weather became normal - rain, thunder and storm stopped. The sky became clear. The starts were seen twinkling as if they were smiling at Larry. An air of comfort was felt blowing over the village. The rain washed the dirt of the village making it pure for a great cause. Everyone in the village felt relaxed.

Larry washed the plates and dishes and kept them in kitchen.

"Larry! Larry! Laarrryy!" called her mother.

"Yes mom." – said Larry politely.

"Wash your hands properly and polish our shoes neatly and cleanly and it must shine." – ordered Mrs Steffina.

"Yes mom. I will polish them." – replied Larry in a suppressed reluctant voice.

"Polish them now." – ordered Mrs Steffina in her usual harsh tone.

"Yes, Yes … mom." – replied Larry.

She washed her hands and took the shoes of her mother and brother and started polishing them. Soon she polished the shoes nicely and indeed they were shining.

She did it well to please her mother with a high positive expectation of winning her favour to get little more food at night. After polishing the shoes she ran to her step mother to inform her that all the assigned tasks were done well.

"Mom, shoes are polished and they are shining." – said Larry with a smile.

"Ok. Keep them there." – she ordered.

Larry kept the shoes on the specific place pointed by Mrs Steffina.

"Mom. Mom, will you please give me something to eat? I am very hungry." – requested Larry quietly.

"Always hungry! You don't have any work apart from eating. I am not cooking anything tonight. We are going for a party tonight. I will give you some cookies. And stay at home – I mean in your room." – she said indifferently.

"Can, Can I please come with you? I am afraid. No electricity – it is too dark." – requested Larry in a beggar's voice.

"How dare you to ask me to join us in the party. You don't deserve that. You will look anomalous with us in party. You nasty girl better stay at home!" – said Mrs Steffina with crossed face and her eyes seemed to be turned red.

Larry knew the consequence if she had dared to persuade her more. Instead she gave up and left. Larry went to her room in the stable. It was quite dark. Still little thundering sound could be heard and lightening could be seen. Larry was very much afraid. As soon as she entered the stable she could see the nymph was waiting with a candle light and her room was looking very nice as the nymph had decorated it nicely and the horses were also seemed to be happy after seeing Larry as if they also wanted to wish her –

"Happy Birthday Larry."

Larry felt good. Happiness tried to fill her heart but she could not express her happiness.

"Welcome home! Miss Larry, wish you a very happy birthday." – said the nymph cheerfully.

"Thank you… thank you. What should I call you?" – asked Larry.

"You can call me Marolina. I am Marolina Mafushi." – replied the nymph.

"Oh yes Marolina! Very nice decoration! It's beautiful. First time I am seeing such beautiful decoration in my room. I am very glad to see this. I am very happy." – said Larry with a happy heart hiding aside her hunger.

"Wait Larry we will make it gorgeous very soon and we will celebrate your birthday with a grand party. Many of your real friends will come tonight to meet you. You are our princess!" – said the nymph.

"Princess! I am princess?" – asked Larry surprisingly.

"Yes you are the princess." – replied the nymph.

"But I am not the daughter of any king. How can I be a princess?" – asked Larry being confused.

"Yes you are! You are the princess of Syndriya. Your mother was a noble witch and a just queen who assured justice for all her subjects." – said the nymph proudly.

"No she was not a witch. My mother was a lovely mother. She was not a witch – she was a very lovely wonderful woman." – said Larry in protest.

"You were brought up by Lady Kathleen, the kind hearted woman – she was not your real mother. She got you in the mountain jungle in a wretched condition. She saved you and adopted you as her own daughter." – said the nymph.

"You are lying …" – said Larry and before she continued the nymph started –

"Your mother was a queen. She established justice in the turmoil state and led the people to lead an honest life. She ruled Syndriya justly and became the apple of eye of all witches and wizards and the people used to love her a lot. But the evil witches of Izyndriya became jealous of our happiness, peace and prosperity and started attacking us. Very soon they started destroying us, our land and properties. Your mother tried her best to save her land and people but failed as the evil queen of Izyndriya cheated her and we left Syndriya in search of a safe abode. (suddenly the nymph stopped for a moment and there was a complete silence) … Oh I am sorry I am not allowed to say this to you." – said the nymph.

"Marolina please tell me more about my mother. I want to know about Syndriya." – asked Larry curiously.

"I will tell you later dear. Have little patient. You will come to know everything soon." – said the nymph.

"No please tell me now. Please …" – requested Larry.

The nymph was not permitted to say all these secrets related to Larry's life to her. By mistake the nymph told her. As Larry was trying to force the nymph to know more about her mother. The nymph was trying to avoid Larry.

"See Larry tonight after midnight you will turn ten and you will meet many of your friends. You will come to know your true identity. You will receive some magical power and revelation. So be patient for few more hours to know all these things." – said the nymph to Larry.

"That's fine, but you can tell me now – I am anxious … I am excited to know about my mother and …" – continued Larry but nymph was not ready to share the secrets.

"We are nymphs … we are born servant. We cannot tell all these things to you. If I am caught sharing all these information with you, I will get very hard punishment. Or removal from the wizardry world." – said nymph sadly.

Larry understood his inability. She stopped forcing the nymph to say anything about her mother.

"Ok … I can understand your problem. Don't worry I will not force you anymore." – said Larry.

"I have to go now to arrange your birthday party. I will come back soon." – said the nymph and it disappeared.

It became dark. Larry was left alone in her room … alone in darkness.

Chapter 6 Larry's Birthday Celebration

It was completely dark. After sometimes flash light and thundering started again. Flash light making Larry blind and the deafening sound of thundering was terrorizing. Larry was in great confusion about her own identity. She was totally confused. She was feeling lonely. She was very much frightened. Her empty stomach was crying for food. But she ignored it as she was too much afraid to care for her hunger. She was almost feeling like crying. A drop of tears fell on the floor and started glowing like a diamond in the darkness. Another drop fell and started shining brightly like a diamond.

"Who am I? Why is my tear shining brightly like a gem? They are strange things. The witches whom I have never met earlier are strange creatures. They call me Great Miss Larry Potter. But I am Miss Larry Smith. Someone calls me Princess – Princess of Syndriya! Who I am actually?" – Larry spoke to herself in an utterly confusing state of mind. She was sitting indifferently.

She heard some strange sound. Her heart-beat increased. The pet dog of Larry's family was barking a lot and the pet cat was making strange sound. She came out from her room to see the matter. She could see the two burning eyes of her dog standing in front of the main door and burning two eyes of her cat from the balcony. She was afraid that something strange was going to happen. She heard some strange sound. Though she suspected the sound would be of some strange things but it was the sound of joy and merriment.

"Larry … dear Larry….. Where are you? Your friends are here." - a soft, loving and soothing sound called Larry.

Larry looked at the direction from where the sound was coming but could not see anyone. She got confused.

"Look at me Larry down here." – said the voice.

Larry saw a cat – that black cat and the small height nymph was with it.

"Happy birthday Miss Great Larry Potter! Wish you a happy prosperous birthday." - the black cat and the nymph said together.

"Thank you very much." – Larry replied.

The nymph with its magical power started making a big magical tent for the celebration of Larry's birthday party. It was decorated so nicely that it was looking like a luxurious palace. Larry became surprised to see that her house was decorated so nicely with glowing lights of multi-colours. The nice curtains added extra beauty to the decoration. She could not believe her own eyes. It was decorated as if any royal wedding was going to happen. She was so happy to see this.

"Here is a nice piece of clothes for your birthday party. You please wear this and get ready as soon as possible. Guests are on the way. They all will be here when the clock will strike twelve at midnight." – said the nymph with a smile.

The black cat started uttering some strange words in a forceful voice and continued to shake its body. Soon the black cat turned itself into a beautiful black lady – though she was black but her beauty was appealing.

The nymph and the black lady took Larry to a room for dressing.

"Waw! What a nice dressing room. What a nice mirror!" - exclaimed Larry in surprise. First time in her life she was watching such beautiful things. They removed Larry's old dress to replace it with the new party wear. But Larry's body was very dirty and some bad smell was coming from her body. She was in urgent need of a bath.

"Come, first take a bath with nice rose water and after that use these scents from Arabia. I am sure after that you will like a princess" – suggested the black lady.

The nymph Marolina helped Larry to have a rose shower and after that Malmossie, the black lady sprinkled nice Arabian scents over her body. They helped Larry to get dressed like a princess. Larry wore a nice long dress and covered her head with a nice scarf and put a golden crown over her head and really she was looking like a princess.

"Beautiful! Very beautiful! Gorgeous!" - said Malmossie.

"Gorgeous! Pretty Princess! You are looking like a real princess now." - exclaimed Marolina, the Nymph.

They kissed Larry's hand. Larry looked at her own face in the mirror. She was very happy to see her extremely beautiful face. Her heart got filled with extreme joy.

"Thank you very much Malmossie and Marolina. Thank you so much!" - Larry said to them with a lovely tone.

"You are looking like your mom." - said Marolina.

But Malmossie stopped Marolina to say anything further. They all became busy for the party. The clock stroke twelve. It was midnight. A very nice music was heard. The three witches – Hecate, Kirke and Lilura - arrived on a mat with gifts in their hands. A unicorn appeared with a gorgeous lady riding on it. Another nice lady appeared –

her half body was like a horse with big wings and she was having a bow and arrow in her hand. Many owls and bats came and turned into different witches. Many rats and tadpoles also came and turned into wizards. All sat down on their respective chairs. Marolina and Malmossie took Larry to the stage where a big size cake was kept on which it was written –

"Happy Birthday to you, Great Miss Larry Potter."

The gorgeous lady who came on a unicorn approached towards Larry and wished her – 'Happy Birthday dear Larry'. The half-human and half-horse lady also came to Larry with a smile and wished her – "Happy Birthday".

"Ladies and gentleman!" an announcement was heard.

It was Marolina, the nymph who was anchoring.

"We are very happy to see you all in this grand birthday party of our Princess Larry Potter. You are all welcome. Have a drink and cheer in the name of our princess."

All started saying - "Larry, Larry…Larry… Larry, the great, Larry the Great! Live long. Long live Larry!"

"Thank you very much." - said Larry to the crowd with her natural smile feeling grateful to all present guests.

The crowd became silent.

"I am highly thankful to our reverend lady Great Lyola, the Queen of Glombia for gracing her presence in this auspicious birthday party of Great Miss Larry Potter." - said Marolina pointing to the lady who came on a unicorn.

The nymph turned towards the half-human and half-horse lady and said –

"I am also thankful to our respected lady Great Loreal for arriving in Great Miss Larry Potter's birthday party. She is the most swift and helpful member in our community. I would like to request Great Miss Larry Potter to cut her birthday cake and I request Great Lyola to help her and humbly request Great Loreal to accompany Great Larry Potter."

Larry started cutting her birthday cake and everybody stood up and sang –

"Happy birthday to you, dear Larry….."

Larry offered a piece of cake to Great Lyola and another piece to Great Loreal. In return they also offered her cake. Malmossie cut the cake into small pieces and within a moment it was served to all present members. Larry came with a piece of cake and offered to the nymph and another piece she offered to the black lady, Malmossie. Tears fell down from the eyes of the nymph and the black lady as they first time got the honour – the offer from a princess. They can't control their emotion.

"Dear friends" – spoke the great lady Lyola. She addressed to the audience.

"I am thankful to our Lord that I got a chance to join our savior and protector Great Larry's birthday party. I would like to draw your attention. Please listen to me. Larry has crossed nine – now she is ten years old. And we all know that when she turns 10 years a revelation will appear in her right index finger and she will get great power. Gradually she will become the finest and strongest witch of the world – without a second like her."

"Now I think the old prophecy will become true. Larry is our great hope. She will become the most powerful witch." - claimed Loreal.

All became very happy. A nice music was heard. The three witches started dancing – a wild dance. Larry was hungry but now she felt good and ignored her hunger. She was very happy and content. A lot of colourful live entertaining activities are performed to please all and make the party a grand one. The three witches started a wild dance of strange type. All enjoyed the wild dance of the three witches.

Now it was the turn of another group of witches to sing and dance. Yes they were very happy to sing and dance in Larry's birthday party. They started singing and dancing. Everybody clapped a lot to appreciate them.

After them it was the turn of the wizards. They presented a dance of different taste making everyone feeling like dance. All started dancing. It was awesome. Now very nice smell of multiple dishes can be felt. The nymph announced –

"The dinner is ready. All are requested to settle down in their designated seats and enjoy the dinner."

All the members present in the party started eating the sumptuous meal with great pleasure. Larry first time in her life was having such delicious dishes in her dinner. She was very hungry in the evening but after getting such a great meal she didn't feel that much hunger. The very presence of meal filled her stomach.

"Larry, my dear, eat anything that you like to eat and enjoy yourself." - said Great Lyola lovingly.

"Yes Larry don't hesitate to eat anything or if you wish to have any other dishes tell us, we will bring it for you." – pleaded Loreal with a pleasant tone.

"No, thank you. This is a gorgeous meal. I am eating. Really the meal is great. I like it." - replied Larry.

All became busy in enjoying the luxurious dinner.

Chapter 7 Magical Gifts from Loyla and Loreal

A very ferocious roaring could be heard. All became afraid and silent. A gloomy air flew over the party.

"Is it thundering outside?" – Joe, the rat asked.

"No, it is not thundering." – Malmossie, the cat replied with an anxious tone.

"Ignore it, just enjoy your dinner." – Marolina, the nymph said suppressing its fear.

"No, we cannot ignore it." – Lyola said.

"It is not the sound of thundering – it is she whose name we don't utter. She is roaring. The queen of darkness is roaring." - Loreal said.

"Our Great Larry has turned ten, now she whose name we don't utter will be able to spot her. And she is waiting for this day. Her power will become super-power once she can capture and use our Great Larry's blood and soul." - added Lyola in a warning and anxious tone.

'So we must be very much careful and we all will protect our Great Larry even at the cost of our lives. She is our last hope and she must be protected." - said Loreal.

"We will train our Great Larry to defend herself and to fight against all black evil power. It is prophesized that her death is in the hands of our Great Larry. So she will try to capture and kill our Great Larry as soon as possible but she cannot do it easily as she is not having that much power. She is living a life of parasite. She will send her evil army to kill us … to kill Larry. We must save our Great Larry from all evil power." - Lyola said.

"Good thing is that our Great Larry possessed equal power by birth and can defeat any black evil power and she can do it. Just we have to train her." - Loreal said.

"She is having a strong army of evil witches who are ferocious and heartless. So be aware of them. They can transfer themselves into any animals' form. They might be a great threat to us if we are not careful." - Lyola said.

"Another good thing is that she whose name we don't utter is also in partial captivity like our queen. There is a magic stone that can free them." - Loreal said.

"Our reverend queen is in captivity. She whose name we do not utter had captured our queen and engraved her body alive in some rock and trapped her soul. If we want to free our queen we must find that magic stone. With our queen she whose name we don't utter was also got struck in some rock but her soul escaped only body was struck. She needs Larry's blood to free her body – to incarnate her body and to get back her lost power." Lyola said.

"We must be careful and alert for the safety and security of our Great Larry. She whose name we don't utter will send her best servants to capture or kill Our Great Larry and we must protect her. She is our last hope to get back our lost glory – our lost power – our lost position." - Loreal said.

"We must keep in mind that our first priority is Larry's safety and security." Lyola said.

"We will do our best to save and protect our great Larry." – the crowd of witches and wizards said.

The thundering sound became more fearful and flash of

thunder light can be seen through the veil of the tent. It was a dark night. All cheerful and jolly faces became serious. The party seemed to lose its merriment. Larry also seemed to be more serious and matured but no sign of fear can be traced in her face. Rather she seemed to be ready to face the challenge.

"Attention please" – an announcement was made by Marolina, the nymph.

All became silent and paid attention to the announcement.

"After dinner, some of our well-wishers will present some precise gifts to our Great Larry." - said the nymph and all started clapping.

Great Lyola came with a shining gift box for Larry.

"Here is a small gift from Lyola, Great Larry please accept this." – said Lyola and offered the ring to Larry.

"I heartily accept your gift and thank you very much Lyola." – replied Larry with a great smile and opened the wrapping and exclaimed in joy – "It's a lovely ring!"

"Can I help you to wear this ring?" – asked Lyola.

"Yes please help me to wear this ring." - replied Larry happily and stretched her left hand pointing to her ring finger.

"Neither left hand nor ring finger – you have to wear this on your index finger of your right hand. It is not an ordinary ring. It has special power. Just wear this ring and you will understand the magical power of this ring. Just try and see." – said Loyla instructing all these.

The ring was little weird but you cannot find any sign of magic or weird decoration or any script. But it was looking different from other common rings. Though it was very simple, it was looking gorgeous and stunning. As soon as Larry wore the ring she became invisible. All the members were surprised and happy to see this. Larry can see all and none can see her.

"Larry it is a very precise thing and keep it safely. Be responsible for it and handle it with care. This ring will help you to become invisible." - said Lyola to Larry.

"Really it will make me invisible!" - exclaimed Larry and only her sound is heard.

"Yes dear. It will make you invisible. In fact you are now invisible." - said Lyola.

"Really I am invisible now. I cannot believe. Can I test it whether I am invisible or not?" - asked Larry curiously. Only her voice was heard.

"Yes sure you can. You are now invisible." - replied Lyola.

Larry went to Joe, the rat who had becoame alive with her tears. But she did not find any expression from Joe that could prove her presence. Larry pulled Joe's tail and he hit another rat suspecting that the latter had pulled his tail. So the other rat tried to slap Joe but missed as Joe bent down and by mistake he slapped a cat. The cat became very angry and tried to catch the rat. A funny chaos – the cat after the rat. All were laughing a lot due to this. It added more fun and merriment to the party. The cat kept trying its best to catch the rat but the rat also tried hard to save itself.

All started laughing at their foolish fight.

"Larry are you here? Larry are here?" - Marolina, the nymph announceed.

The cat was about to catch that rat but Larry appeared in front of the cat and saved the rat.

All started laughing again at her sudden appearance and started shouting –

"Larry, Larry, Larry, ..."

"It was my fault. Forgive this rat." Larry requested the cat.

"How it is your fault? That nasty thin rat has slapped me. I will teach him a lesson." - replied the angry cat.

"No. No… it is not his fault. I pulled Joe's tail invisibly to have fun with him. But he thought that this rat has pulled his tail. So Joe hit this rat and this rat tried to slap Joe in return but by mistake he hit you. So please forgive him." - pleaded Larry.

"Ok dear Larry. I forgive this rat." - the cat replied.

"Larry, please come on the stage. Many wonderful gifts are waiting for you. Come as soon as possible." – called Marolina.

Larry hurried towards the stage.

On the stage Loreal was waiting with a nice gift for Larry.

"Here is a small but very powerful gift for you, my dear Larry." - said Loreal and handed over her a magic stick with a star on its head.

"Waw! It shines so nicely!" - exclaimed Larry.

"Need to be more careful, alert and swift with it and it has lot of power. It will turn your wishes into reality. It can burn your enemy. You can do anything with it. Whatever you command, it will do for you." - instructed Loreal with her matured words.

"Really it will turn my wishes into reality!" - asked Larry.

"Yes dear it will do whatever you command." - replied Loreal.

"Can I try now?" - asked Larry with a cute smile.

"Yes you can…… it's yours now." - replied Loreal affirmly nodding her head.

"Serve everyone with a nice drink." - commanded Larry to the magic stick.

Instantly everyone got a nice drink that none had tasted

before and it was really excellent.

"Thank you very much Loreal and thank you very much Lyola for these wonderful gifts!" - said Larry to Loreal and Lyola.

"You are welcome dear. But don't misuse these things on trifle things. Don't use them unless it is extremely necessary. Use them when it is beyond human control. Otherwise you may lose them forever." - warned Loreal.

"And don't apply any magic to your family members and neighbours either to harm them or to benefit them. Don't try to show them that you have special power. Don't ever let anyone know that you possess such things." - warned Lyola wisely.

"Yes I must be careful and I will never do so." - replied Larry obediently.

"One more thing I want to say you that these magic things cannot be seen normally. They always remain invisible. Whenever you need them, you just close your eyes and make a wish for them and they will be with you. Otherwise it will remain invisible all the time. It must be handle with proper care and attention." - warned Loreal.

"The shining magic stick and the magic ring is your property now. We have deadly enemies who want to possess it. So don't share any information regarding these things with anyone. Handle them with utmost care and attention." - instructed Lyola.

"Only you and she whose name we don't utter can use this ring and magic stick. She may be searching them madly. It is you who can better guard and use it." – said Loreal.

DEAR READERS IT IS ABRIDGED VERSION. IF

WANT THE FULL BOOK. PLEASE CONTACT US
AT Email - syedmikailali@gmail.com